THE ADVENTURES OF SQUIRREL AND MOUSE

ALLY MCLEAN

IILLUSTRATED BY ANADINY MOGNO

Thank you.
Scribal Publishing

This Book Belongs to:

Other Ally Books

THE HANNAH BOOKS

Have You Seen My Grandma?
Have You seen My Christmas Angel?
Have You Ever Made a Wish?

THE FAIRY BOOKS

The Bedtime Fairy
The Tooth Fairy

THE ANIMAL FABLES

The Adventures of Squirrel and Mouse

Visit AllyMcLean.com for up to date list of wonderful books.

Or visit my author page:

One fine day, a mouse and a squirrel set off on an adventure. They walked through a forest. They hoped to reach the field on the other side. This field, they'd heard, had an orchard full of delicious fruit.

"What an amazing day!" laughed Squirrel, as he skipped along. "What a wonderful world! This orchard is going to be *fantastic*!"

Mouse smiled. "Maybe; maybe not," she replied. "Let's wait and see."

"Oh, don't be such a stick-in-the-mud," teased Squirrel. "This is going to be fun!"

For though the pair were old friends, they were very different creatures. While Mouse was calm and cool, Squirrel was up and down. He was *always* getting carried away.

The bird snatched Squirrel and Mouse
in her talons. They were carried up and
up and up; through the trees, out into
the open sky.

Just then, the sky grew dark. They
looked up to see a swooping shadow.
It was a Great Horned Owl.

"Oh no!" cried Squirrel. "It's all over!
I'm never going to crunch another apple
or nibble another pear!
Now I'm owl food!"

But Mouse, though clasped tight in Owl's claws, wasn't so sure. "Maybe; maybe not," Mouse shrugged. "Let's wait and see." While Squirrel struggled and panicked, his bushy tail waved in the air. It tickled Owl's nose.

"Ah – ah – ah – CHOOO!" sneezed Owl.
It was such a big sneeze, she let go of her
lunch. Mouse and Squirrel were free.
"Hooray!" cried Squirrel happily. "Here we come,
apples; here we come, pears! We're safe!"

"Maybe; maybe not," said Mouse, the wind
ruffling her fur as she fell. "Let's wait and see."
"What's there to worry about?" the Squirrel
asked, laughing.

Mouse pointed down at the treetops. They were getting nearer and nearer and nearer. Squirrel realized that he was plummeting through the sky!

"Disaster!" he cried. "Calamity! Squirrels
aren't meant to fly! We're going to crash
into a tree! Or thud into the ground!"
Mouse scratched her nose. "Maybe;
maybe not," she said. "Let's wait and see."

They didn't crash into a tree. Nor did they thud into the ground. Instead, they plopped into a pond, making a very large SPLASH!

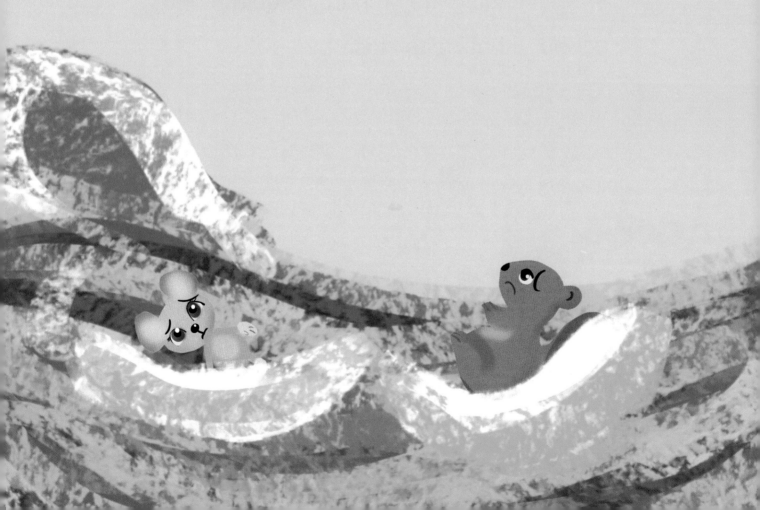

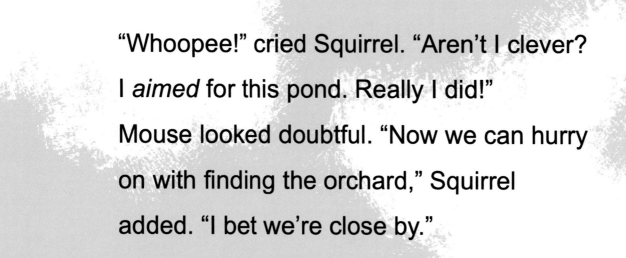

"Whoopee!" cried Squirrel. "Aren't I clever? I *aimed* for this pond. Really I did!" Mouse looked doubtful. "Now we can hurry on with finding the orchard," Squirrel added. "I bet we're close by."

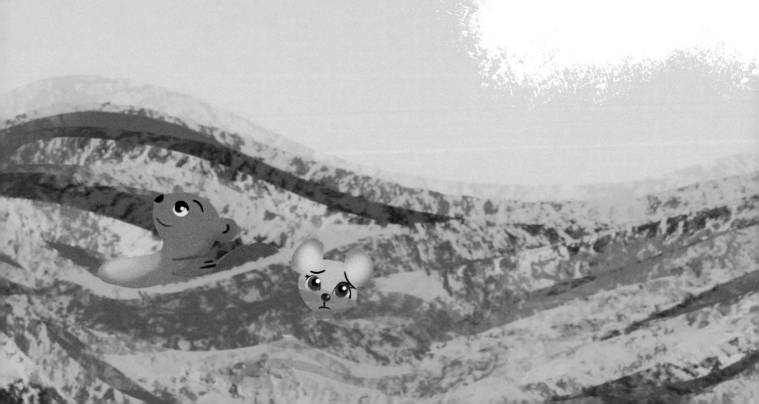

Mouse coughed out some water. "Maybe; maybe not," she said. "Let's wait and see." From deep in the pond, they heard a rumble and a grumble. "What's that?" the squirrel asked nervously, before …

… a gigantic fish burst from the water. Opening its jaws, it swallowed them in one gulp. Mouse and Squirrel found themselves in the fish's belly.

"Yuck!" Squirrel cried out. "This is *disgusting*! It's dark and wet and smelly!" It was all too much for poor squirrel. "We should never have left home," he sobbed. "Now we're stuck and there's no way out!"

Mouse put an arm around her friend's shoulder. "Maybe; maybe not," she said, with a comforting smile. "Let's wait and see."

At that moment, the fish began to fly through the water. It went faster and faster. Then, to their surprise, it was hauled into the air.

"What on earth?!" yelped Squirrel. "What's happening?!"

The fish had been caught by a fisherman!
Now it dangled on the fishing line, while Mouse
and Squirrel rolled to and from inside its belly.

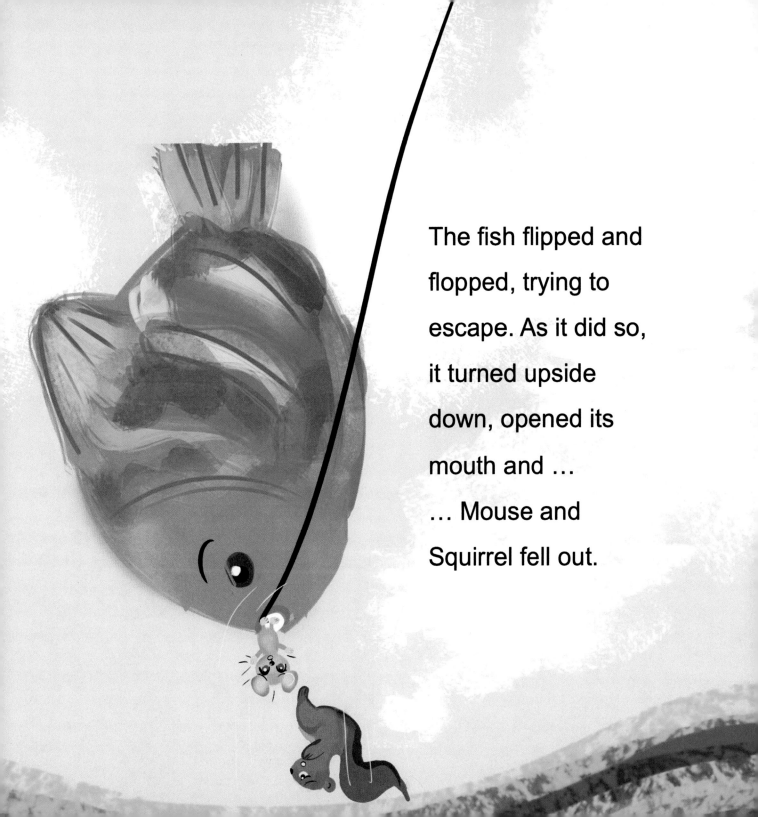

The fish flipped and flopped, trying to escape. As it did so, it turned upside down, opened its mouth and …

… Mouse and Squirrel fell out.

They landed with a splat on the muddy bank. Shaken and confused, they shook themselves dry. "Ha ha!" laughed Squirrel. "We're alive! We're ALIVE! I *told* you there was nothing to worry about."

"Maybe; maybe not," said Mouse, wringing her whiskers dry. "Let's wait and see." They padded down the little path through the wood. Light shone through the trees. Birds sang. Leaves rustled in the breeze.

After a while, they reached the end of the path. They stepped out from the forest into the bright sunlight. Before them, fields and meadows spread out beneath a bright blue sky. It was beautiful.

"Now," said the Squirrel, grinning, "where's that orchard?" He rubbed his paws together. "It's going to be the BEST THING EVER!"

Mouse smiled at her friend.

"Maybe; maybe not," she said.

"Let's wait and see."

Questions for You

Stories are fun and they can also teach us something.
What are some of the things this story taught you? What else did it teach you?

We all respond to situations differently.
Do you think you respond more like Squirrel or Mouse? What has you say that?

Sometimes unexpected things can throw us off.
How do unexpected things make you feel? How do you react to things going differently than you wanted them to?

When we get emotionally upset, it helps to have things we can do to make us feel better.
What are some of the things you can do to help yourself feel better? What else can you do?

A Gift For You

Thank you for purchasing The Tooth Fairy. As a way to say thank you, I offer you this FREE coloring book version for your little ones to enjoy. Please type this link into your browser to download your gift: AllyMcLean.com/squirrelandmouse

Returning Wonder to Reading!
Ally McLean

THE ADVENTURES OF SQUIRREL AND MOUSE

ALLY MCLEAN
ILLUSTRATED BY ANADINY MOGNO

A Review Would Be Sweet!

I hope you enjoyed reading, *The Adventures of Squirrel and Mouse.* Your feedback is very important. I'd be so grateful if you took 3 minutes to go back to Amazon and leave an honest review. Your review really matters!

Returning the Wonder to Reading!
Ally McLean

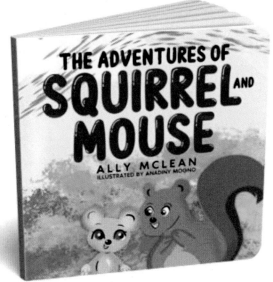

About the Author

Ally McLean is a beekeeper, gardener and small business owner. Influenced by her father, Ally fell in love with books at a young age and became fascinated by how myths, legends and epic tales shape our lives. Her dream is to bring joy and wonder through reading to youngsters and adults alike.

Made in the USA
Monee, IL
10 August 2022

11355307R10021